This book belongs to:

Jojo

and

the

Incredible

Ask

written by

Shameran Hanna

illustrated by

Katerinka Rudenko

1

It was not long ago, in late December, that a miracle took place – one to remember.

It all started when I made a wish. Not for a toy, or a pet, but one that just fit. Inside the house, next to the tree, I sat by the fireplace and whispered quietly,

"Dear Santa, all I want for Christmas is to say words clearly. I've got one thing on my list: to be able to speak like everyone else, and just as quick. I can't find my words, and I can't say them fast enough. It makes me sad, and it makes talking tough. I want to recite a rhyme, and say it out loud, and not feel flustered, but confident and proud."

3

"Ok, kids, it's time to write your letter to Santa!" my mom announced. My siblings ran over from the other side of the house. "I want a doll, and a purse to go with it," my sister insisted. My brother shouted, "I want a bulldog with a spiked collar; I'll name him Tiger, and we'll play for hours."

"Well, son," my mother advised, "be careful what you wish for, because you just might get it; and you need to make sure to take care of it, and feed it, and pet it." Just then, suddenly, everyone looked at me. Here's all I could say, and all I could think:

"Uh…I, I, I want…a…toy!" I responded with a smile and a wink. But Santa knew what I'd written in the note; he knows what I think. We folded our letters and sealed them with excitement, then left them by the front door, ready to be sent.

That night, all three of us slept by the tree – my brother, my sister, and me. When over at the fireplace, I heard a shuffle, I sprang up from my sleep to see what was the trouble.

"What was that?" I said out loud. Everyone was sleeping, no one awake to be found. Out from the garland that was spread across the mantle, emerged a tiny figure – magical in nature. I knew in a moment that it was an elf. Even with his small stature, he quickly climbed down from the shelf.

"Ring a ding-ding," he said to me.

"You…you…can…speak?" I stuttered.

"Yes, I can…speak," he mocked me. He had a sense of humor, and it kind of shocked me.

"I don't have much time. My name is Morty, and I'm here to chat about your wish to Santa."

"I…I just wish I could speak like everyone else, just as clear and quick. There is nothing more I ask for this year from Ol' Saint Nick."

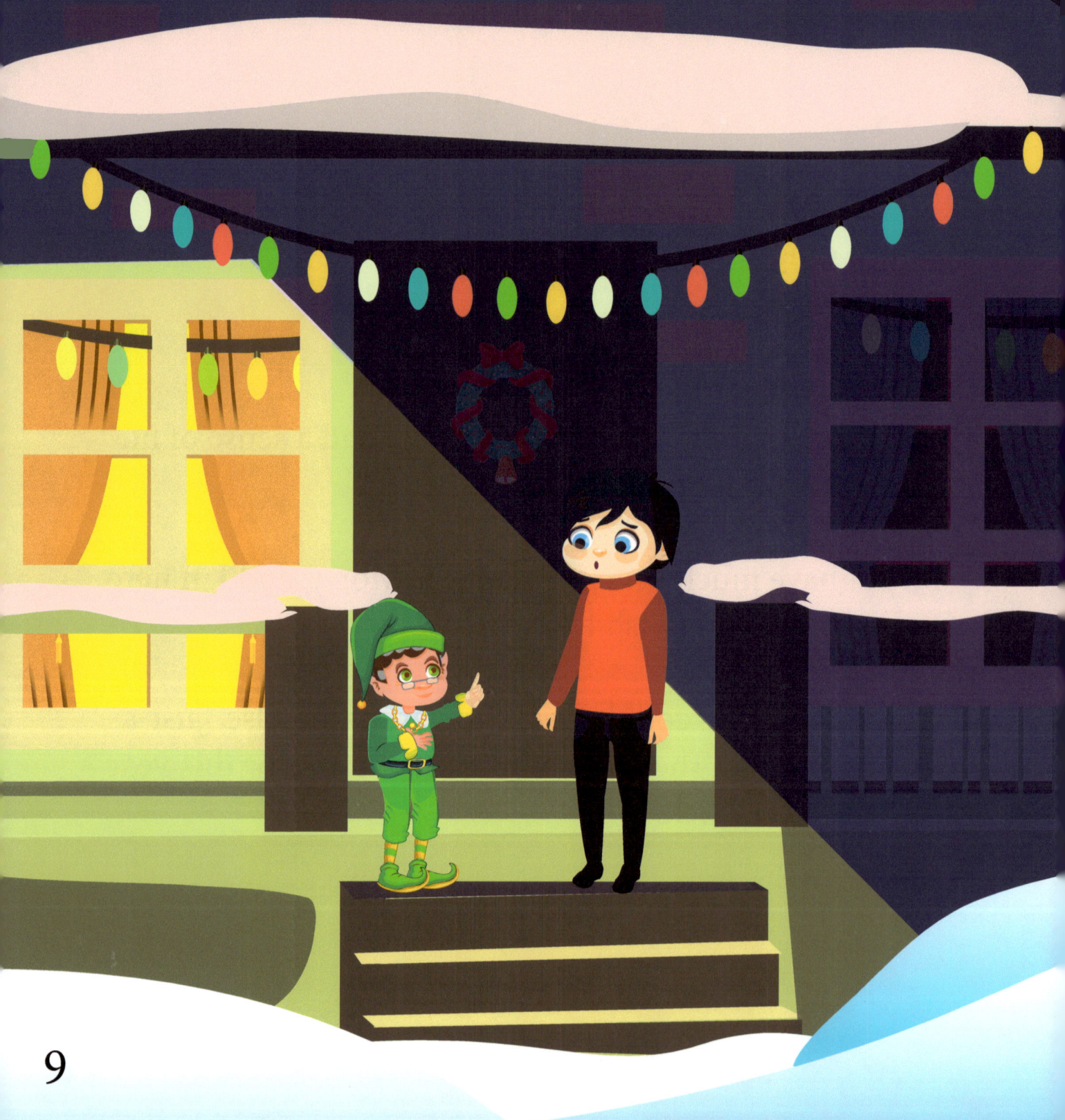

Morty the Elf walked toward the front door. He asked me to open it and stand on the porch. "I want you to know that what you're asking for…it's not a doll or a pup, a trinket, or a toy. Your wish can be granted from within yourself. Jojo, you can make that happen, not Santa or an elf. Now listen to me. I want you to close your eyes and take a deep breath. Think of the next word you would like to say. Imagine the word in your mind before you say it."

(*Readers take a deep breath.*)

As we stood outside on that cold winter's night, I took a deep breath as I wanted to recite… But then I forgot! My words, my thoughts! What was I going to say, and what was my point? I ran back inside and slammed the front door, angry that I couldn't think anymore. "There's no use! I'll never be able to recite a Christmas poem or say grace!" And just like that, Morty the Elf vanished without a trace.

11

Christmas Eve came by just like a flash. I wasn't sure I'd get my wish. I was nervous, in fact. The house filled with friends and family, and with plenty of laughter, food, and candy. Upon the dining table lay a feast of food. As my mother looked at me, she announced to the entire room:

"Jojo, can you say a few words about Christmas?" And I, in my surprise, and I, in my fright, stopped to think for a second, took a deep breath, and then began to recite:

"And, lo, the angel of the Lord came upon them, and the glory of the Lord shone round about them: and they were sore afraid. And the angel said unto them, Fear not: for, behold, I bring you good tidings of great joy, which shall be to all people. For unto you is born this day in the city of David, a Saviour, which is Christ the Lord."

With cheers and applause from the crowd, I realized I was not stuttering, but reciting out loud! I said every word loud and clear. I'd done it! I'd done it this year!

From the corner of my eye, I thought I saw Morty the Elf run between the sea of people and out the front door. I chased him outside and looked around. Nothing was there but something sticking out of the ground. Fallen from the mailbox was my letter to Santa, which had never been mailed out.

"Ring a ding-ding." I heard a voice behind me. Perched on top of the roof were Morty and his tiny reindeer. "I don't understand. Why wasn't my letter sent out as planned?"

"Mistakes happen, kid. Looks likc that plan was canned. But your wish came true. You didn't need Santa to read that letter. You believed you could, so YOU made yourself better. Just know that everyone has challenges to work through. Yours just may take a second or two. Nobody is perfect, don't be so hard on yourself. Take it from me; I'm a fun-sized elf! Even though I'm small, I can build the biggest toys of them all!"

"Morty, are you from New York City, by chance?"

"Me? No, I'm from the North Pole, and I'm just trying to be the best elfin elf I can be."

15

When Christmas came, my sister got a doll, and my brother got a puppy. There was a box left with my name on it; how'd I get so lucky? Lo and behold, inside the box was an electronic microphone, with a note attached:

"You can have all the toys in the world fall into your lap, but confidence is the best thing you can unwrap."

Just then, I heard the sound of sleigh bells ringing outside. "Ring-a-ding-ding" echoed through the sky. I looked out the window, as it would appear, a tiny elf and his tiny reindeer.

I heard him exclaim as he drove out of sight: "Batteries not included, so charge the mic overnight!"

Make your own Morty

Color, cut out, and tape together your own Morty!

Tag us on Instagram #MortytheElf

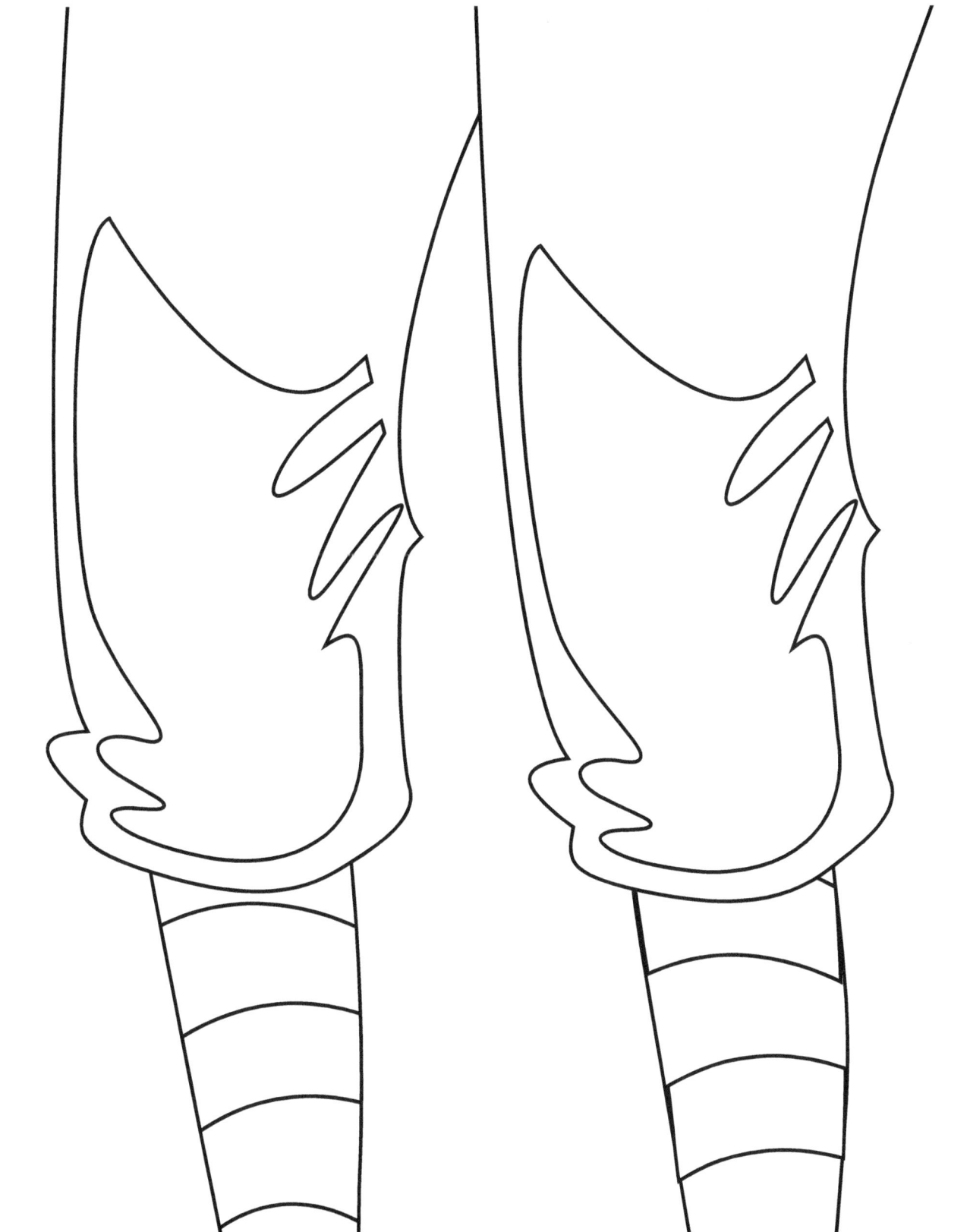

www.ingramcontent.com/pod-product-compliance
Lightning Source LLC
Chambersburg PA
CBHW041007170626
46815CB00002B/200